SmartGurlz

Adventures

Table of Contents

Chapter 1.

Jun : The Chic Geek

Jun popped another shiny, green gummy bear into her mouth before she put the plastic bag back in her stylish brown leather back pack. She slipped it over her shoulder and then clicked the strap of her helmet.

With a gentle kick she flicked her scooter's kickstand back into place and turned on the engine of her cherry red metallic Siggy scooter.

She was happy that she was tall for her age and looked slightly older than 15 years old because she technically wasn't legally allowed to be driving her scooter.

She did have her learner's permit but with careful

driving and a bit of luck she had managed to get by without any problems.

She smiled to herself, 'Ok, I am a bit of a rebel' and pushed forward through the Honey Locust tree-lined streets of the Upper West side in Manhattan– the fresh, cool wind whipping through her hair.

Her summer in Italy had been incredible.

That was where she had learned how to weave in and out of crowds skillfully on her small scooter.

And no one there cared if she was under 16 and driving. Everyone had funny, little scooters in Rome. She missed driving through the aging cobblestone streets, eating Amerena cherry gelato ice cream and walking among the crumbling historical buildings all around her.

Often she attached a GurlPro camera and video to her scooter and would take the most adventurous videos of her driving adventures.

Sometimes she pretended she was Audrey Hepburn in Roman Holiday, zipping around town, reading maps and devouring ice cream cones.

She had felt so lucky to be accepted to the Foundation League Science Camp that was held just outside of Rome, in the tiny white-washed town of Sperlonga.

Topped upon a cliff overlooking the sea, Sperlonga was a short ride from the city and boasted an archaeological museum, on the site of Emperor Tiberius' ancient grotto.

The camp was known worldwide for being the 'best of the best' and Jun had spent her summer studying organic chemistry from world renowned scientists.

Sperlonga was the perfect location for these studies. Organic chemistry or as her friends call it – O-Chem is about all living things, both plants and animals, that are made out of molecules that have carbon in them.

And Sperlonga had some pretty amazing plants and wildlife to discover and analyze.

Not only did she spent the summer studying what she loved but she also got to learn how to bake her favorite treats from the Italian chefs at the camp after her lab sessions.

That was her other hobby. Baking. For her, it was like a delicious form of chemistry.

She got to mix things and taste their reactions. And now that she was heading to her best friend Lisa's house, she was armed with her organic chocolate almond biscotti, a recipe she had perfected that summer.

The kitchen was a disaster and she didn't want to know what her mother would say when she saw it. But Jun had somewhere to be. NOW.

She left a note saying "Sorry about the kitchen mom, Love you! Ciao, Jun ".

She knew that wouldn't help much though but at least her Mom would be happy she started using some Italian words like 'Ciao' which means goodbye and pronounced like 'Cheow'.

Her best friend from high school was math brainy like Jun. She had graduated this spring with Jun even though she was just 16 years old.

She had been accepted to Stanford University with a scholarship and was moving to California to start school in the fall, which was actually just a couple weeks away.

Jun knew that she was going to miss Lisa so much when she started her first semester at New York Institute of Technology (or N.I.T) and she secretly wished that Lisa would change her mind and transfer to the same school.

But she knew Lisa. Lisa was way too excited for the yellow, sandy stretches of beach and flip flops all year round.

Jun sped over to see her friend and to have one final sleepover before they would part ways.

Chapter 2:

Bye Bye BFF

When she got to the door, Lisa opened it before she could knock and smiled sadly. Lisa would miss Jun too.

'Buongiorno bellissima,' said Jun with a smile and a gummy bear wedged between her teeth.

'One summer in Italy and now you speak Italian? You didn't eat all the gummies did you?" Lisa said with a wink.

"Nope, I only had one!" Jun said with a laugh.

They went inside. Lisa's mother was busy packing up some things for Lisa's new dorm room and was talking to herself under her breath. Jun nodded at her and Lisa just rolled her eyes.

"Her baby is going off to college." Lisa said in a mock whining tone. "Come on, let's go up to my room and you can show me your pictures from Italy. I just got a new USB cord so we can hook it up to my computer."

Lisa said as she pet the large cat that stood on the stairs. Lisa's cat, Tubby, had chewed through the last cord and looked proud of it.

Jun patted him on the head as they marched upstairs to Lisa's room.

The whole place looked like a wild tornado had gone through it. Lisa's clothes, shoes, lap tops, cables and suitcases were everywhere.

She had a few boxes packed but very few clothes had actually made it into the open luggage.

Jun just laughed and shook her head. Lisa had always been like that.

She would start something then get distracted by a

science project, a new computer program or technology experiment and would get lost in thought for hours. It was the price of being such a brilliant tech girl. Jun would miss her chaos nonetheless.

Lisa sat down at her laptop and plugged in Jun's smartphone. Then she brought up her favorite software for viewing photos and videos.

As a tech girl, Lisa had access to the best software and this program had fantastic resolution and had some creative tools to use so that Jun could edit, crop and even add filters.

Jun pulled up a stool from the corner and started describing what was happening in the pictures. Lisa was soaking it all in and dreaming about going to Italy herself.

"See that one there? That is just around the corner from the Coliseum." Jun said pointing to the screen.

"It's a pigeon Jun." Lisa said unimpressed.

"Yes, it's an Italian pigeon!" Jun said with a giggle.
Lisa started laughing too. She knew Jun was
fascinated by the strangest things.

Fortunately, the pigeon was sitting next to a beautiful
little fountain so the picture wasn't a total loss.

"OK. Moving on. Some of these need to go on
Facebook and your blog" Lisa said as she clicked and
clicked. Jun went through each photo and carefully
described everything that led up to her snapping the
picture.

She painted the story as best she could because she
knew that Lisa desperately wanted to go to Italy.

Instead of going on a European adventure, Lisa had
spent the summer at nearby Camp Wakinaya where
she wasn't allowed to do experiments or play with
any technology. The camp even required her to not

bring her smart phone, tablet or laptop.

She even had to leave her mini-drone in the car.

Her parents had sent her there to give her a "normal summer experience" before she went off and started school.

They were proud of Lisa in their own way but she knew that they didn't really understand her. At least, not the way she needed them to.

They knew she was special but they still tried to get her to act like a normal 16 year old.

Jun was grateful that her parents had always been encouraging of her going into science.

Her mother was a top biologist and was a renowned lecturer in physics so math was popular topic at home. Her parents even let her build a chemistry lab in the basement of their house.

Sometimes late at night, Jun was bustling about with

googles on and adding chemicals into beakers, flasks, test tubes with her bunsen burners blazing away.

She was glad that she would be able to stay with them for the first few years of college. She was keenly aware that she would be the youngest student at N.I.T.

Lisa, on the other hand, was very happy to move away from her parents and the New York City.

Lisa often complained about the crowds, the stinky subway and the bitter cold winters.

California was definitely the place for her. When Jun finished showing her the pictures they went to sit on her bed.

They talked about the classes that they were signing up for and when their orientation started. That's when Lisa's mom came in and looked at the mess of a room.

"Lisa! How are you going to have this all packed by tomorrow? It's a disaster in here! Let me tell you missy, I am not packing this for you." She said with a huff then turned to walk out of the room. Then she turned back and walked in to give Lisa a big hug and said, "I am going to miss you so much!"

Jun and Lisa were both stunned by the rollercoaster of emotions coming from her mother.

When her mother left, Lisa widened her eyes and turned to Jun and said, "Craaazy. She's been like this since I got back from camp."

Jun grabbed her soft leather backpack. She looked at it critically, it was a vintage beauty, she thought to herself. She had picked it up in Italy and she couldn't wait to snap a photo of it and place it on her blog, Chic Geek.

"Organic biscotti?" Jun offered with a silly smile as she grabbed the cookies out of her bag.

They both laughed. Jun helped her pack a little and then the rest of the night was spent watching cheesy romcom movies and stuffing their faces full of greasy pepperoni pan pizza and Haribo gummy bears.

Jun told Lisa stories about authentic crispy, thin Neapolitan Italian pizza cooked on stones covered in fresh tomatoes and basil and Lisa licked her lips.

They fell asleep on the floor of the living room to the sound of The Sisterhood of the Traveling Pants movie.

Chapter 3:

Jitters Before School

The next day, Jun gave Lisa a big hug goodbye and they promised to text every day, post on Facebook and see each other when Lisa came back for holidays.

But as Jun drove back to her house on her scooter, she felt strange. Cutting through Central park, she entered her neighborhood littered with immaculate brownstones, five-floor walkups and charming little French restaurants and luxury shops.

It was a feeling she hadn't had in a long time.

She was nervous.

She had been planning on going to university in the fall all year.

She had toured the campus and chosen her classes and was very happy to say goodbye to her high school.

But somehow she had ignored how big this was. She was going to college and she would be the youngest one there….

When she got home she was greeted at the door by her very annoyed mother, Ivy.

She had cleaned the messy kitchen and was ready to yell at Jun for being so irresponsible when she saw Jun's face and stopped.

"What's wrong, honey?" her mother asked.

Jun looked at her with a strange expression and said, "I guess I am just going to miss Lisa… I hadn't really thought about what it meant for her to move away until now… and I am nervous for school…"

Her mother hugged her and said, "What happened? You were so excited."

Jun shook her head. "I don't know mom… It's just… I guess I hadn't really understood what it meant to start college. I'm just glad that you'll be here with me." Jun said with a weak smile.

Jun's mom gave her a big hug and a kiss on the head.

"You will have a great time sweetie. The other students will be older and know more so they will give you more of a challenge. '

'And I am sure you will find great friends who are just as passionate about science as you are." Jun's mother said soothingly. "Oh and Jun, your father and I are very proud of you."

Jun nodded and smiled at her mother.

Then she walked to her room and pulled out her laptop and started writing on her Facebook blog, Chic Geek.

She hadn't written on her blog for a few days but felt like she needed somewhere to put her emotions. She laid on her bed and grabbed her favorite green neon fuzzy pillow.

Changes....Something happened and I don't know what. Maybe it was saying goodbye to my best friend, L. But now I am really nervous about school. What if I don't make any friends like her? What if people still make fun of me because I am young and live with my folks? What if I am still a nerd? Or worse... what if I am not as smart as the other students? I still want to be a neuro-chemist... maybe when I graduate I will understand the chemicals in my brain that are causing these emotions.....

Italy was so easy. It was easy to make friends because

everyone there was into science as much as I am but no one had to be a genius to be there. I felt like I could be myself and no one would judge me. I wonder if others are worried about this stuff too… I wish I could make something that would give me courage for the first day.

Well, for now I suppose I can do only one of two things… I can bake or I can hunker down in my chemistry lab.

That's all for now.

Yours,

J

Chapter 4:

It's All About Chemistry

Jun looked around her room and saw her newly purchased Chemistry book that was for Chemistry lab 101.

She pushed herself up off of her bed and grabbed it then headed down stairs to the basement.

When she got to her lab she put on her goggles and opened the book. She decided the best distraction was to do each experiment in the book from start to finish.

At least that way, she would be able to keep up in that class with the students who were two years older.

She always felt better in the lab. She was in control in the lab. The room was organized and had beakers of all sizes. She had her own microscope and her parents had just bought her a white lab coat that she would wear all the time if she could.

Happily, Jun grabbed the supplies and chemicals she needed and put on her gloves. And away she went!

The next day was new student orientation and school would start the following Monday.

Jun rode her scooter across the Brooklyn Bridge and into the southern part of the city where the N.I.T. campus was located.

She parked near the auditorium and pulled out her campus map and itinerary for the day. Each student had been emailed the day before so they all knew where to go.

To Jun's surprise, she saw a lot of the other students walking with their parents.

She felt a little better knowing that she was independent enough to be there on her own but she also felt like she was just pretending.

She hoped no one would ask her how old she was.

As she walked into the large auditorium she was asked for her name and photo ID by an upperclassmen who was standing at the door.

As she handed him her permit card he eyed it suspiciously then looked her over. He knew she was 15. Then he checked his clipboard for her name.

He actually looked surprised to find her name on his list but, with a grumpy look, he motioned toward the doors.

"Ok Jun. You need to head in these doors and take a left. You will find the line for your school ID.'

'By the way, make sure you are ready once it's

your turn because you don't get to take more than one picture,' he yelled after her.

NEXT!" He said and motioned for the girl standing behind her to step forward.

Jun took her ID and walked inside.

The lobby was full of students and Jun felt the familiar wave of nervousness wash over her.

Then she saw the line for the Student IDs and stood at the end. She wished she had worn a different outfit.

Instead of wearing her favorite sundress and pearl earrings, she had decided on jean shorts and a T-shirt because she knew she would be walking around campus a lot and worried she would stand out in nice clothes.

And now this outfit would be in her picture for the next four years. 'Great... ' she muttered to herself.

She tugged at her shirt nervously and thought about what the other girls in line were wearing.

She was comforted that most of them had shown up in similar outfits. But as she looked at their faces she was amazed.

They all looked calm and seemed so prepared. And most of them were at least two years older than her. They were women. She became more convinced that she wouldn't fit in easily.

The line moved pretty quickly and before she knew it, it was her turn. She sat down and smoothed out her hair. Then there was a flash.

"NEXT!" Shouted the man behind the camera.

Jun was handed her new ID card and the picture was awful.

She had been mid blink when the camera flashed and her head was at a funny angle.

She slouched and dragged her feet as she walked, feeling defeated before the orientation had even started.

She mindlessly grabbed a new student welcome bag and found a seat that was far from anyone else then stared at her ID.

She didn't look up until she heard a noise from the stage.

"Hello. Testing… one, two… one, two…" Said a very chipper voice.

Jun looked at the stage to see a very upbeat looking woman who obviously worked for the school.

"Hello everyone! Welcome to N.I.T. Orientation!" She said enthusiastically.

The whole room applauded and Jun clapped along.

"Now, everyone please find a seat so we can get started." Jun listened to the rustling of students trying to find a seat and the empty seats around her were filled with eager looking students.

"OK, so, like I said, this is Orientation for new students for the class of 2019! We are so glad to have you here and we know that the experiences you have at N.I.T. will mold the rest of your lives. If you will all take out your itineraries that we emailed to you yesterday, you will see the schedule for the rest of the day. '

'In a few moments, I will turn the mic over to the University President and then we will hear from a couple of our professors and student counselors. '

'After the program here, you will all be split up into groups and given a tour of the campus guided by upperclassmen who are happy to answer any questions you may have. Then we would like to welcome you all to a nice spaghetti dinner at the cafeteria." The cheery woman turned and nodded at a man off stage and then spoke again.

"Ok, please help me give a warm welcome to the University president!"

She said and clapped her hands together. The audience of new students clapped softly as the man in a suit walked onto the stage and took the microphone.

"Hello. I want to extend my warmest welcome to you,' he said as he looked around the room.

'You are here because you are the best and brightest students of science that your generation has to offer. '

'I am sure that with the help and direction of the professors here, you will all go on to contribute a great deal to the science of the future,' he continued.

'Look around you. The person sitting next to you could be the next Steven Hawking or Neil Degrasse Tyson. The people around you are now your peers. They will challenge you and support you every day. '

'You will watch them grow into the men and women of science and I have no doubts that there are people in this room that will change the world.

'So know that this school is tough. We expect excellence and integrity from every student. But if you do your best, there is no reason why you should not reach your goals. Thank you."

He said in a very serious tone.

Jun thought about what he said.

She still felt nervous but she also felt a new sense of belonging.

This is where she needed to be. This is where she was meant to be.

She smiled to herself as she listened to the student advisors talk about class schedules, course loads and social pressures.

She knew all this already and wondered if there was someone else in the room who hadn't dealt with these struggles in high school.

She had planned out her courses carefully so that her first semester would be on the lighter end and she could figure out how much more work she could take on.

She knew herself, she knew what she could handle. And as for "social pressures".

She wasn't worried about drinking at parties, she had always thought that was a waste of brain cells, she was just worried about making friends.

But all of the speakers seemed pretty confident that everyone would make friends so Jun tried to believe them.

Finally, there were two speakers that were actually interesting.

The first was a female Chemistry professor who had a research lab on campus and the second was a professor that split his time teaching and working as a neurobiologist.

Jun sat forward and stared at them as they talked about their fields and how they had gotten interested in science.

The chemistry professor talked a little longer and Jun was glad she did because of what she said.

"You know, when I was getting into college, it was pretty rare for a woman to be interested in Chemistry. I struggled with my peers because they thought that I wouldn't be able to contribute as much as they could to the field. But I was fascinated by chemistry and math. I loved testing reactions and being in the lab. With a lot of work and refusing to give into the pressure around me, I was able to graduate at the top of my class and now I get to do what I love for a living. I am happy to see that there are a lot more women in the audience today but I can easily see that you are still the minority. There have always been more men in these subjects. But I am here to say, welcome. You can and will do great things! I am happy to usher in a whole new class of women in science. Thank you." She concluded.

Chapter 5:

Struggling To Be The Girl

Jun was beaming.

She had struggled a little in high school. All of the other kids that were interested in Chemistry were boys and they definitely had not made her feel welcome.

They made fun of her when she went in after school to use the lab just because she was a girl.

They asked her why she didn't just go to the mall and play with makeup.

Though Jun did like fashion and makeup, she was very serious about science. The worst part was that one of the science teachers, Mr. Fredrick, didn't stop them or say anything.

That had made her really mad. But she had pushed forward with her dreams and worked hard.

It had paid off. All of those boys were still in high school and not doing too well with their classes.

Jun looked up to the speaker and was happy to be one of the girls in the audience who were making a difference. And she was making a difference just by being there. She loved that.

When the program ended, Jun stood up and stretched her legs.

She filed out of the row of chairs just like everyone around her and then tried to find her group.

The lady who spoke at the beginning of the program had told them that they would have their groups assigned to them by a number that was written on the bottom of the welcome bags.

Jun lifted her bag to look at the bottom to see a number written in big black letters.

21.

That was her group number.

Jun pushed through the crowds until she saw a sign with the number 21 on it and a tired looking student standing under it with bluish rings under his eyes.

She walked up and was about to tell him her name when he held up his hand.

He motioned like he was counting heads then suddenly said, "Group 21 follow me and don't get separated."

Jun followed him outside with ten other students.

He pulled them off to the side and they sat down on a patch of grass. "Ok let's quick go around and say names and what we are planning to study. My name is Jim and I am a junior studying Mechanical Engineering. Now you."

He said pointing to the girl sitting on his right.

"Oh uh, I am Maria and I want to study architecture." Said the beautiful girl. She had long, black wavy hair and high heeled black boots on.

She gave off an artistic vibe and Jun couldn't help but stare at her. She had the coolest tank top on with what looked like a half completed Sudoku grid on it. Fortunately, Maria just smiled at Jun. Jun smiled back and blushed a little.

Next was a shy boy who Jun could barely hear even when she leaned in. Everyone in the group gave each other funny looks and they moved on.

Sitting next to him was a blond girl who was fiddling with a small gadget in her hand.

"Oh, me?" She said. "I'm Jen. I want to study Mechanical engineering." She said as she held up the little gadget in her hand. The blond girl next to her looked at the device with great interest before jumping in.

"Hi, I'm Freja and I want to study aerospace engineering." She said with a smile.

The guy next to her was staring at the intelligent blond next to him like she was an alien. Finally she nudged him and he introduced himself.

"I'm Max and I want to study Biology." He stuttered. Next it was Jun's turn.

"Uh, I am Jun. I want to study Chemistry… and maybe biology." She said nervously. She blushed when they all looked at her.

She was so flustered that she didn't hear the rest of the student introductions.

Jim led them around the campus, showing them each where the main buildings were, where the school gym was and where the libraries were.

He pointed out interesting things along the way that Jun knew that she would forget but listened with interest anyway.

She made a special note when he showed them the best place to get coffee and pastries. Finally they ended up outside the cafeteria. It was dinner time and Jim disappeared.

The girl named Maria walked right over to Jun and stuck out her hand. "Hey, Maria. Jun right?" She asked as she shook Jun's hand.

"Yea, I... I love your boots." Jun stuttered. Maria smiled and then rolled her eyes. Jun suddenly became worried, did she say something weird?

Chapter 6:

New Friends and Fresh Air

"Are you nervous?" Maria asked thoughtfully and Jun sighed then nodded. The other two girls walked over to them.

"I'm nervous too… but I figure, making friends will help us get over that." Maria said.

Jun doubted that Maria had ever had problems making friends.

The other two girls laughed and said, "Hey, can we get in on that too?"

And just like that Jun felt an enormous weight being lifted off her shoulders.

She had three other girls with her who felt the same way she did. She wasn't alone.

They all walked in to the cafeteria together and loaded up their plates with pasta.

Then they found and empty table and started to get to know each other.

They talked about their hobbies and Jun was amazed to find that these girls were just as into science as her.

Of course, they had different interests than her but they were really incredible.

Maria was an artist and drove a el-bike. Freja wants to be an astronaut and already knew how to fly a plane! And Jen, she built her own el-scooter.

Jun couldn't help but notice that these incredibly smart girls that she was talking to were all beautiful each in their own way and were obviously very fashionable.

Most people thought that girls in science had to be 'plain' and not be interested in girly things.

Jun was excited to know that she wasn't the only girly girl who loved science.

After talking for hours, the new friends said goodbye and Jun jumped on her scooter.

She drove home in the twilight lit streets and smelled the familiar scent of New York City in August.

She was so excited about her new friends and felt so lucky that she got to go to school in such a beautiful city.

When she got home she poured out her welcome bag on the bed and grabbed her diary. She sat in front of the pile of things that were all coated in N.I.T.'s school colors.

She had pens, pencils, a couple notepads, post-it's a t-shirt and a pair of flip flops. Jun pulled the N.I.T. t-shirt over her head and leaned back against her pillows. With her new N.I.T. pen, she began writing in her diary.

Dear diary,

Today was orientation. There were a lot of students and a lot of speakers. Most of them were pretty boring but there were two speakers that I really liked. It felt like they were talking only to me.

They convinced me that I can do this. That I can be a Neuro-chemist or Neurobiologist... either one.

There was one who was a woman and a scientist. She said she had problems getting into science just because she was a woman. It reminded me of those jerks in high school that made fun of me. But she kept going. Even when it was hard. Now she has her own lab at a university! I think she is going to be my role model for the next four years.

After the orientation, (which was super long), I met up with a group outside and we walked around the campus. I think it will take me a couple days to memorize the campus layout but I am pretty good at directions and navigation so I am not worried.

The guys in our group were a little weird. Maybe it was because there were so many girls or because the girls were really impressive… or maybe 18 year old boys are just weird… in any case, I think I will wait to date anyone until I know that they aren't all strange…

And good news! I made friends. Already!!! I met three girls in my group and they are so cool! We have a few classes together this semester and I think we are going to get together to study. Now I am so excited for classes on Monday. I can barely sleep… I think I will pick out my outfit for the first day and pack my bag. Mom bought me the most beautiful messenger bag to carry my books in! Eek!

All for now.

Yours,

J

Jun jumped out of bed, turned on her favorite music and danced around her room as she went through her closet.

She grabbed a sundress that she had bought in Italy. It was very flowery and had lace straps and trims.

It was about knee length which was perfect for riding her scooter. She grabbed some strappy yellow and cork wedges. Then for the final touch, she grabbed her thin white, leather jacket.

Then she bounced around as she packed her bag and then grabbed her campus map. She looked it over and planned the best route to take between her classes.

The weekend went by so slowly that Jun was anxious the whole time. She moved a mile a minute and baked up a storm with cranberry orange scones.

She was going to bring pastries for her new friends when they met for coffee on Monday morning.

And when Monday morning came, Jun walked into the Java Script coffee shop in her new outfit and baked goods.

The smiles from her new friends made her feel ready to take on the world.

Made in the USA
Las Vegas, NV
18 July 2022

51786090R00026